Bad Luck, Dad

Written by Catherine Coe

Illustrated by Erin Taylor

Collins

T0321815

Dad dips the rod in.

2

I hop up. A fin!

Dad tugs the big rod.

4

Dad gets a big cod.

Dad tugs the rod. No!

Dad lets the cod go.

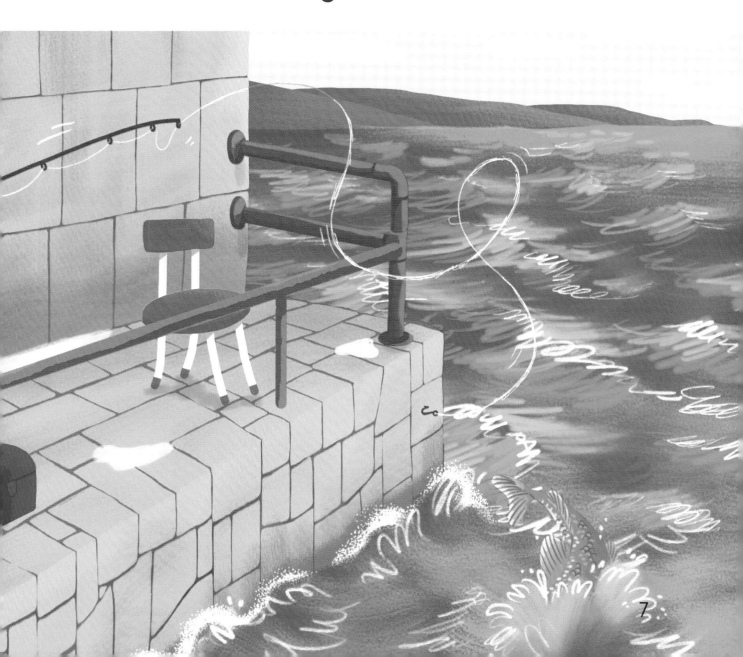

Dad huffs and Dad tuts.

I tell him bad luck.

As the red sun sets,

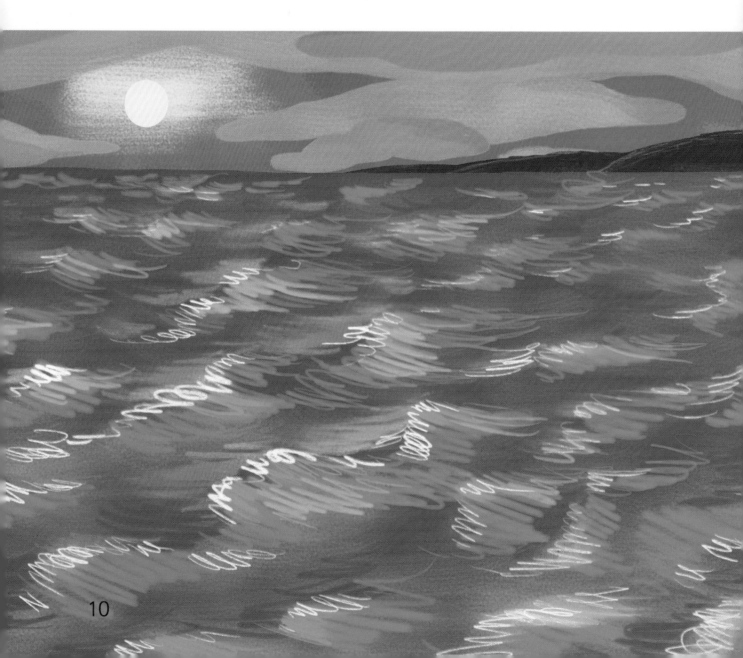

I kiss and hug Dad.

I pick up the rod.

Dad can get a cod!

/l/

ll

14

After reading

Letters and Sounds: Phase 2

Word count: 60

Focus phonemes: /g/ /o/ /c/ /k/ ck /e/ /u/ /r/ /h/ /b/ /f/ ff /l/ ll ss

Common exception words: as, the, I, no, go

Curriculum links: Understanding the World: The World

Learning objectives: Listening and attention: listen to stories, accurately anticipating key events and respond to what they hear with relevant comments, questions or actions; Understanding: answer 'how' and 'why' questions about their experiences and in response to stories or events; Reading: read and understand simple sentences, use phonic knowledge to decode regular words and read them aloud accurately, read some common irregular words

Developing fluency

- Your child may enjoy hearing you read the story.
- You could take turns to read a page, modelling reading with lots of expression.

Phonic practice

- Point to the word kiss on page 11. Sound out the word. As you say the sound /k/, put your finger under the letter 'k' and then do the same with the letter 'i' as you say the sound. When you get to the /ss/ draw a line with your finger under 'ss' to show that that 'ss' represents one sound. Now ask your child to do the same.
- Now do the same with the following words:

  huffs   h/u/ff/s (page 8)   tell   t/e/ll (page 9)   pick   p/i/ck (page 12)

Extending vocabulary

- Turn to pages 14 and 15 and ask your child to find actions in the image that use the sounds /l/ /ll/ and /ss/ (e.g. *pull, luck, laugh, miss*)
- Ask your child if they can think of another word that could be used instead of **dips** on page 2. (e.g. *dunks, puts, drops*)
- Ask your child if they can think of another word that could be used instead of **gets** on page 5. (e.g. *catches, traps, grabs*)